THIS BLOOMSBURY BOOK
BELONGS TO

....

FEATURING...
(in no particular order).

Chaffinch

Barn Owl

Greenfinch

Song Thrush

Dove

Chiffchaff

Mallard (drake)

House Martin

Domesticated Duck

Swallow

Pigeon

Blue Tit

Blackbird

House Sparrow
(female)

Woodpecker

Jay

Starling

Robin

House Sparrow
(male)

Turkey

Peacock

for Ben
thank you
xxx

Bloomsbury Publishing, London, Berlin and New York

First published in Great Britain in 2009 by Bloomsbury Publishing Plc
50 Bedford Square, London, WC1B 3DP

Text and illustrations copyright © Sarah Dyer 2009
The moral right of the author/illustrator has been asserted

A CIP catalogue record of this book is available from the British Library

Hardback ISBN 978 1 4088 0218 2

1 3 5 7 9 10 8 6 4 2

Paperback ISBN 978 0 7475 9998 2

3 5 7 9 10 8 6 4

Printed in China by South China Printing Company, Dongguan City, Guangdong

All papers used by Bloomsbury Publishing are natural, recyclable products
made from wood grown in well-managed forests. The manufacturing processes
conform to the environmental regulations of the country of origin

www.bloomsbury.com/childrens

The Girl with the Bird's-Nest Hair

Sarah Dyer

BLOOMSBURY

LONDON BERLIN NEW YORK SYDNEY

Hollie was just like lots of girls,
she did not mind her messy curls.
Hollie did not like her hair being brushed,
much to her mother's utter disgust!

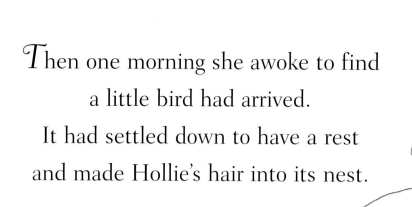

Then one morning she awoke to find
a little bird had arrived.
It had settled down to have a rest
and made Hollie's hair into its nest.

Her mum, however, was not so sure,
she was worried there might be more!
"You cannot keep it," said her mum,
"just in case more of them come."

Soon enough a second appeared,
which was as her mum had feared.
"I should give my friends a good feed,
we must go and buy some birdseed!"

As they went off to the shops,
birds gathered in the treetops.

Two little birds soon became nine.
But Hollie thought all this was just fine.

In the supermarket while Hollie's mum bought pizza and bread,
Hollie's friends flew round her head.

"Your hair is becoming a bit of a crush.
I think now might be time to give it a brush."
Hollie replied, "Absolutely no way!
All these lovely birds are here to stay."

Later that day, they went off to the farm.
Hollie took birdseed tucked under her arm.

While at the farm they stopped for some cake
and Hollie's mum cried out, "For goodness' sake!
It's gone on too long – I must brush your hair,
there are birds absolutely everywhere."

"No, Mum," said Hollie. "It's perfectly fine.
These little birdies are simply divine!"

So off they went around the farm
and Hollie's mum tried to stay calm.

PIGGY

COW

While Hollie was feeding a cow and a pig,
her mother was worried that the birds were too big!

On through the farm Hollie skipped, gathering pace.
By now though, her hair was running out of space.

With her mum chasing and waving a brush at her hair,
Hollie continued, completely unaware
that behind her were turkeys calling out, "Gobble gobble".

Jumping on to her head, they made Hollie wobble.
But that was nothing compared to what was to come
as Hollie cried out for her comb and her mum.

For behind her a peacock leapt into the air
and landed right in her messy red hair!
Obviously this all came as a bit of a shock,
there really was no room for a large peacock!

As Hollie lay there, squashed on the floor,
she couldn't avoid it, not any more.
"You can brush my hair now, Mum. I've decided to give in,"
she said, looking up from the ground (with a cheeky grin).

SPOTTED!

Chaffinch

Barn Owl

Greenfinch

Song Thrush

Dove

Chiffchaff

Mallard (drake)

House Martin

Domesticated Duck

Swallow

Pigeon

Blue Tit

Blackbird

House Sparrow
(female)

Woodpecker

Jay

Starling

Robin

House Sparrow
(male)

Turkey

Peacock

Also by Sarah Dyer . . .

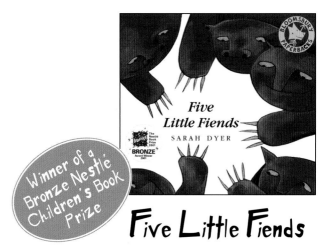

Winner of a Bronze Nestlé Children's Book Prize

Five Little Fiends

"A picture book which approaches perfection"
Financial Times

Clementine and Mungo

"Touching tale of sibling love"
BBC Parenting Magazine

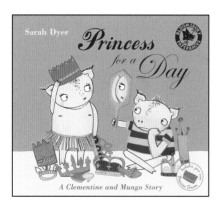

Princess for a Day

"A must-read for just about every three- to five-year-old female"
Observer